SESAME STREET®

Take Us to the Ball

GRUMP-IRE
NOW
SCRAM!

By Constance Allen
Baseball card text by Jodie Shepherd
Illustrated by Tom Brannon

A Random House PICTUREBACK® Book

Random House  New York

"Sesame Workshop,"® "Sesame Street,"® and associated characters, trademarks, and design elements are owned and licensed by Sesame Workshop.
© 2018 Sesame Workshop. All Rights Reserved. Published in the United States by Random House Children's Books, a division of Penguin Random House
LLC, 1745 Broadway, New York, NY 10019, and in Canada by Penguin Random House Canada Limited, Toronto, in conjunction with Sesame Workshop.
Pictureback, Random House, and the Random House colophon are registered trademarks of Penguin Random House LLC.
rhcbooks.com
SesameStreetBooks.com
www.sesamestreet.org
Educators and librarians, for a variety of teaching tools, visit us at RHTeachersLibrarians.com
ISBN 978-1-5247-6824-9 (trade) — ISBN 978-1-5247-6825-6 (ebook)
Designed by Diane Choi
MANUFACTURED IN CHINA
10 9 8 7 6 5 4 3 2 1
Random House Children's Books supports the First Amendment and celebrates the right to read.

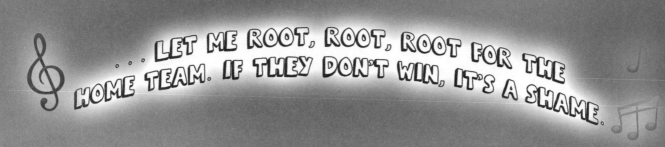

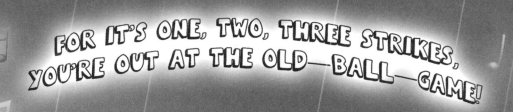

WE WEAR A UNIFORM AND A HAT. WHEN ONE TEAM'S FIELDING, THE OTHER'S AT BAT. OUR FANS ROOT, ROOT, ROOT FOR OUR OWN TEAM. IF WE DON'T WIN, THAT'S OKAY...

LET ME ROOT, ROOT, ROOT FOR THE HOME TEAM.
IF THEY DON'T WIN, IT'S A SHAME.
FOR IT'S ONE, TWO, THREE STRIKES,
YOU'RE OUT AT THE OLD—BALL—GAME!

Remove the team trading cards by tearing carefully along the perforations. Keep them all or trade with friends.
Remove the Sesame Street Sluggers poster by tearing carefully along the perforations, and hang on a wall.